ONE MEAN ANT

For Lavie
Once a neighbor, forever a friend

A. Y.

For Lynn and Nick

S. R.

Text copyright © 2020 by Arthur Yorinks
Illustrations copyright © 2020 by Sergio Ruzzier

First edition 2020

Library of Congress Catalog Card Number pending
ISBN 978-0-7636-8394-8

19 20 21 22 23 24 CCP 10 9 8 7 6 5 4 3 2 1

Printed in Shenzhen, Guangdong, China

This book was typeset in ITC American Typewriter.
The illustrations were done in pen and ink and watercolor.

Candlewick Press
99 Dover Street
Somerville, Massachusetts 02144

visit us at www.candlewick.com

ONE MEAN ANT

written by
Arthur Yorinks

illustrated by
Sergio Ruzzier

CANDLEWICK PRESS

Once, there was an ant.
A really mean ant.

I mean he was so mean, leaves would fall off trees when he walked by.

He was so mean, grapes would shrivel and turn into raisins when he looked at them.

This ant, this mean ant, was so mean that dung beetles would . . . well, never mind what they'd do, they'd just do it when he was around.

Brothers and sisters, this ant was *mean*!

One day, this mean ant was so busy minding everyone else's business, walking around yelling, "Hey, you, dig that hole! And you over there, pick up that crumb!" that he never noticed he had wandered and was soon thoroughly and totally . . .

lost.

"Where the jalapeño am I?" he wondered.
He looked around.
Nothing.
He walked a little to the right.
Nothing.
He walked a little to the left.
Nothing. No trees. No bushes. No nothing.

The mean ant found himself lost in the desert, all alone.

"This sure-'n'-tootin' is somebody's fault!" he shouted. "That's right. You heard me. I'll get you for this!" he yelled to no one.

The ant ranted and raved. And got thirsty.

"What? No water? There's no water in this stinkpot place?" asked the ant. "Dollars to donuts, this must be—"

Oh, he didn't just say *that*, did he?

Well, there the mean ant sat, under the sun, roasting, trying furiously to fan himself, when out of nowhere a fly flew by and landed next to him.

The ant glared. The fly buzzed.

"Fly," said the ant, "I don't understand a word you're saying." The fly buzzed again.

"Perfect," said the ant. "I'm stuck in the middle of nowhere with a fly who doesn't even speak Antish." The fly inched closer.

"Hey! What do you think you're doing? Don't come near me," warned the ant. "You hear me? One more step and I might bite your, uh, I just might bite your, well, I might bite *something* if you come any closer."

"Do you come here often?" the fly asked in perfect Antish.

"What the —!" the ant exclaimed. "You speak my language? How . . . ? Wait a minute. Do you have any idea where we are?"

"No."

"Well, that makes two of us. We're lost!"

"Oh, I'm not lost," said the fly. "I just used to be someplace else, and now I'm here."

The ant started shaking like he was going to explode. "DO YOU HAVE A BRAIN?" he yelled.

"Of course I do," said the fly. "I . . . think."

"You *think*?" asked the ant.

"I think I have a brain. And if I think — well, then I must have a brain," replied the fly. "Uh, I think."

"Oh, leave me alone," said the ant. "And think of THIS with that fly brain of yours. We're in the desert with no food or water and if I wanted to I could just shmush you and have you for dinner!"

"I accept," said the fly.

"What?" asked the ant.

"I'll come to dinner, be glad to," answered
the fly.

"I didn't invite you to dinner!" yelled the
ant.

"You don't have to yell, just because you
have a bad memory," said the fly. "You just
said you wanted to have me for dinner."

"UGH!" the ant cried. "I meant *eat* you for
dinner!"

"Oh," said the fly. "Well, I wouldn't eat you for dinner. Not that I eat much. I eat like a fly. You see, I am a fly, which is why I eat like a fly—"

"Quiet!" The ant was so frustrated he did backflips. "I can't concentrate."

"On what?"

"On getting out of here."

"Why?" the fly asked.

"I'm not talking to you anymore," the ant said, and stuck something out at the fly. I'm not sure it was a tongue, but whatever it was, it was mean.

"You don't have to be so nasty," said the fly.

"Buzz off!" said the ant.

"Sticks and stones will break my bones —"

"You don't have bones!" cried the ant.

"Who says?" asked the fly.

"QUIET!" said the ant.

There was silence.

For three seconds!

"I love waffles, don't you?" the fly announced.

"What?" said the ant.

"Have you ever eaten a waffle?" asked the fly.

"Stop talking!" said the ant.

"I once landed on this big waffle in a restaurant and —"

"STOP!" the ant pleaded.

The fly did not stop. "I have never tasted anything in my entire life that was so delicious. You really should try one."

"AAARGH!" the ant exclaimed. "I've had it!" He began to dig in the dirt and then stuck his head in the hole, his little ant behind waving in the air.

"Wow, I can't do that," the fly said. "You know, I — hey, what's that?"

"What's mut?" said the ant. He actually said, "What's what?" but with his face in the dirt, it sounded like "mut."

"I don't know what mut is, but there's something sticking in your side."

"Well, mut mit it?"

"I don't know," said the fly. "Maybe I can —"

"Don't touch knee! Don't fome near knee, you cuckoo-brain!" the ant said, but with his head still in the dirt, it came out a little strange.

The fly ignored what the ant was saying, especially since he wasn't sure what he was saying, and with his little pincers he pulled a piece of a pine needle out of the ant's side.

"I'll bear your mings off, I'll—" the ant was yelling in the dirt. "I'll . . ."

"Oh!" The ant wriggled his head out of the hole and turned to the fly. "I feel, uh, um, what's that word?" He probably wanted to say "good," but it wasn't a word he used all that often.

"Let's see," said the fly. "You feel . . . thankful?"

"No!" said the ant. "Don't push it."

So there they were, the fly and the ant, baking in the sun, both not saying a word, until the ant turned his whole body around and faced the fly.

"All right," mumbled the ant. "Thank you," he whispered.

"So, uh . . ." the fly began. "So, are we, like, friends?"

"Friends! I, I . . ." the ant stammered. He looked at the fly and, truth be told, he had never had any friends.

"Yeah, okay, I guess, I suppose, maybe, kind of, uh, sort of, friends," said the ant.

"Great. Let's get out of here," said the fly.

"What do you mean? We're stuck here," said the ant.

"Oh, no, I can fly us out of here." The fly flapped his wings a little to show off.

"Are you *kidding* me? All this time you could have gotten us out of here? What is wrong with you?" The ant was upset. "What is wrong with you?"

"You said that already," said the fly.

"If you don't get us out of here in two seconds, I'll —" The ant was very upset.

"Are we still friends?" the fly asked nervously.

"I'll think about it!" cried the ant. "Now get us out of here!"

The fly grabbed the ant around his middle,
and they both rose into the air.

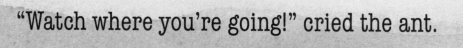

"Watch where you're going!" cried the ant.

"Relax," said the fly.

"*Relax?* There's a—there's a—" the ant screamed.

"I see it. I have eyes, you know," said the fly. "I have lots of eyes. Do you know—?"

"WATCH OUT!" the ant yelled.

"Oh, don't be such a nervous Nellie!" said the fly. "It's a gorgeous day and, uh, um, uh . . .

"W-w-what could go wrong?" stuttered the fly.

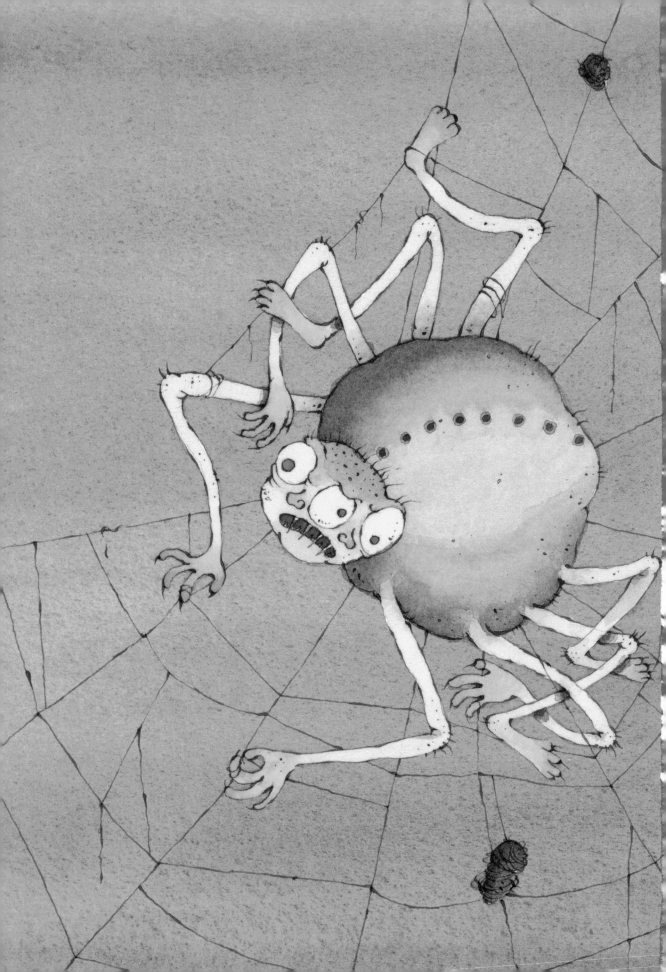